Jacqueline Held · Arnaud Laval · Fabian the Fish-boy

An Addisonian Press Book

First published in the United States 1976, by Addison-Wesley
Printed in Switzerland
Copyright © 1975, Artemis Verlag, Zurich, Switzerland
First Printing
ISBN: 0–201–02895–6   LCN: 75–7538

Fabian the Fish-boy

Written by Jacqueline Held

Illustrated by Arnaud Laval

Addison-Wesley

Fabian wanted to be a fish. . . .

Fabian and his parents lived on the island of Farnholm,
between the sea and the vineyards in a fishermen's village.
He had always played with the fishes,
as long as he could remember.
The grown-ups would not believe it, but so it was:
the crabs, the sardines and the funny little soles
loved him so much that he was almost part of the family.
When he came down to the beach, a sardine called,
"Oh, there is Fabian, the fish-boy!"
"Yes, there is Fabian, the fish-boy!" said the lobster.
"Fabian! Fabian! The fish-boy! The fish-boy!"
repeated
     the haddock and the salmon,
        the herring and the mackerel,
          the eel and the tuna,
            the halibut and the turbot,
              the plaice and the cod.

But in spite of all this, Fabian the fish-boy was not happy.
He did not approve of his father's going out to sea
with his boat each day to catch Fabian's fish friends.

And that's why — as soon as
his father turned his back —
Fabian threw back into the sea:
the haddock and the salmon,
the herring and the mackerel,
the eel and the tuna,
the halibut and the turbot,
the plaice and the cod.

And besides, his mother could say
as often as she liked,
"Fabian is just like a fish
in the water."
It was and always would be
just words.
Fabian knew only too well
that he was not a real fish. . . .

Because real fishes do not have to leave
the sea in the evening and
run,
    sit down,
        blow their noses,
            scratch behind the ear,
                eat from a plate,
                    sleep in a bed,
                        go to school,
and — they do not pull the cat's tail.

So Fabian made up his mind one day to pay a visit to Watawakuda,
the whale, king of the sea. "Oh, Watawakuda, with your black
head and your black tail," Fabian said to him, "what shall I do? I
so much want to be a fish!" Watawakuda, the whale, was highly
astonished and wiped his forehead with his black fin. Such a request
had never been put to him before, and he felt rather embarrassed.
"This, to my knowledge, is the first time . . . ," he pondered, "that
a boy has ever wanted to be a fish . . . the first time . . . hmm . . .
hmm . . . the first time . . . ," he repeated, to gain time.

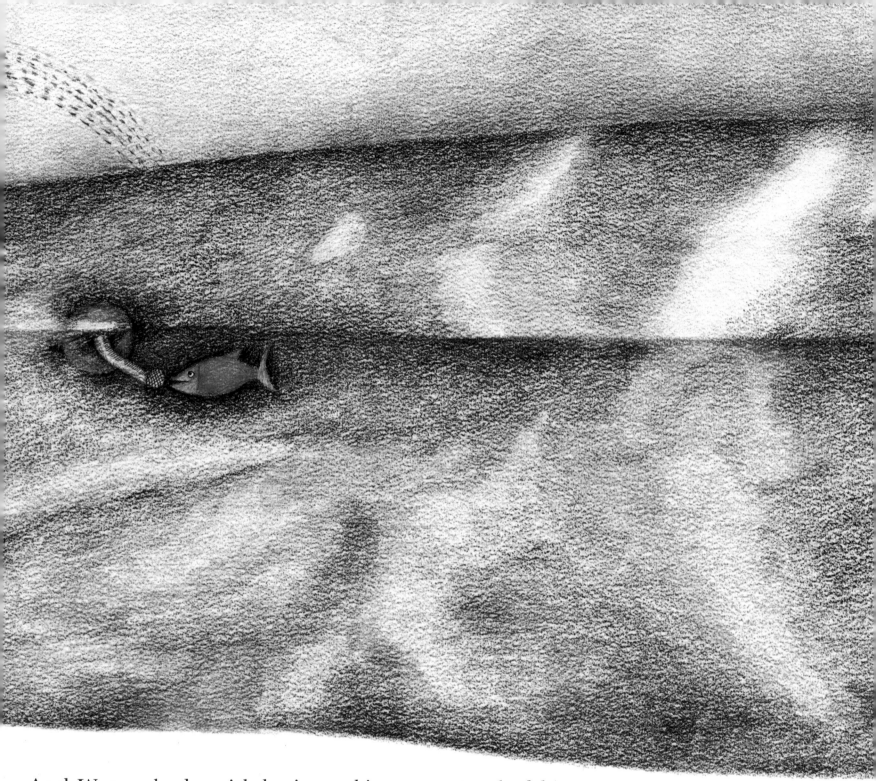

And Watawakuda, with brains as big as a nut, asked his secret
counselor, Fudschi-Fidschi, the pilot fish, what to do.
"I have heard a lot about this little boy," whispered
Fudschi-Fidschi, his secret counselor, into his ear.
"As far as I know he seems to be almost part of the family,
and thus you cannot say no. But, we have to find scales for him."
"We have to find scales for you," Watawakuda, the whale with brains
as big as a nut, repeated to Fabian and fanned his tail fin
to look important.

And then they all came
from the depths of the sea:
the haddock and the salmon,
the herring and the mackerel,
the eel and the tuna,
the halibut and the turbot,
the plaice and the cod —
the multitudes of fish which Fabian
had freed from the fishing nets.

Each fish gave Fabian a scale, and the very generous ones
gave him a fin.
When he had put on his scales and fins, Fabian felt
changed into a real fish.

But what a strange-looking fish he was!
He had big scales and small scales, long scales and round scales,
smooth scales and rough scales.
Whenever Watawakuda, the whale, looked at him, he burst into
laughter.

For a few minutes Fabian felt unsure of himself and the cod
had to show him how to use his fins. But Fabian
was very talented, and all who saw him only half an hour later
had to believe that he had not always been a fish.
"It really is a pleasure to give away some of one's scales
to such a nice little boy," the cod told the plaice.

And now Fabian really thought of himself as a real fish.
But this was not quite right because his funny nut-brown eyes,
sparkling mischievously, remained the same, and they were
the eyes of a little boy, once and for all. And his tousled,
rumpled little-boy's hair still stood up
on top of his head like brown feathers.

He was and always would be a fish-boy — nothing else!

When he did not come home for supper, his father and mother
were very worried.
"Oh, I hope he has not drowned," his frightened mother said.
And his father walked down to the beach and shouted
as loud as he could, "Fabian! Fabian!"

And far out in the sea Fabian heard his voice.

And because he was kind, Fabian wanted to assure his parents
that he was safe and happy.
And because he was polite, he said, "Goodbye for a little while"
to all his friends:
     the haddock and the salmon,
        the herring and the mackerel,
           the eel and the tuna,
              the halibut and the turbot,
                the plaice and the cod.
And he did not forget Watawakuda, the whale, with brains as
big as a nut.
But when Fabian came to the shore, he could not get out of the water
because he was a fish, and his father did not recognize him.
So Fabian, the fish-boy, sat bolt upright on his tail fin,
shook his fish-scales and said in his fish-voice,
"Good evening, Father. It's me. Fabian."
His father was speechless. He just could not believe it!
But when he looked at him closely, he said to himself,
"This fish has indeed the eyes of my little boy. The same
nut-brown, green-speckled eyes like Fabian.
The same untidy, tousled hair."
And again Fabian sat bolt upright on his tail fin,
shook his fish-scales and told his father in his fish-voice
what had happened. His father did not think it was at all funny
to have a little fish-boy who could
not run,
     not sit down,
        not blow his nose,
           not scratch behind the ear,
              not eat from a plate,
                not sleep in a bed,
                    not go to school,
and — not pull the cat's tail.

"Look here," Fabian's father said. "I think it is time this nonsense came to an end and that you turned back into a boy again." But Fabian sat bolt upright on his tail fin, shook his fish-scales and said in his fish-voice, "No, no. I have thought about it carefully. I prefer to stay a fish." And flip, flop, flap he was gone and swam happily away.

So his worried father walked home and asked his wife what to do. His wife thought a minute and then she smiled and said, "But of course! You have to promise him something. Something nice. Something he really likes."

So his father thought of something nice and he walked down to the beach again. "Fabian! Oh, Fabian!" his father called. "My Fabian, if you promise to become a little boy again, we'll give you some nice lollypops." Fabian stood bolt upright on his tail fin, shook his fish-scales and said in his fish-voice,

"No, no. I have thought about it carefully. I really do not want to become a boy again. I prefer to keep my shiny scales." And flip, flop, flap he was gone and swam happily away.

"Oh, my dear wife, what shall we do?"
asked his father.
"Promise him a sack full of marbles. A sack full of big marbles," said his mother.
And so his father went back to the beach.
And it started all over again.
"Oh, Fabian! Fabian!
Please become
a little boy again.
Then you'll get a sack
full of marbles.
Big colored marbles."

Fabian stood
bolt upright
on his tail fin,
shook his fish-scales and said
in his fish-voice, as before,
"No, no. I have thought about it carefully.
I really don't want to become a boy again.
I prefer to keep my shiny scales."
And flip, flop, flap he was gone
and swam happily away.

The situation had become serious!

But then his mother remembered how often Fabian
had begged his father not to catch any more fish.
And since his father was at a loss what to do,
he went back to the shore and called,
"Oh, Fabian! Fabian! If you will become a boy again,
I will not be a fisherman, nor go out in my boat
to catch the fishes ever again."

And Fabian, who loved his fish friends more than anything
in the world, realized that he had to accept *this* offer
and turn into a little boy again.

He stood bolt upright on his tail fin, shook his
fish-scales for a last time and said in his fish-voice,
"I will ask Watawakuda, the whale, for permission."
And flip, flop, flap he swam away to talk to Watawakuda.
But this time he was not happy at all!
"Watawakuda! Oh Watawakuda! With your black head
and your black tail, if I agree to become a little boy once more,
my father promises never to go fishing again."

Watawakuda thought to himself, "Human beings never
know what they want . . . no, they really do not."
But after having consulted Fudschi-Fidschi, the pilot fish,
his secret counselor, he permitted Fabian to leave.

And so Fabian changed into a little boy again.
And his father kept his promise.
He did not go out to catch the fishes anymore
but worked in the vineyards,
and in summer he took people out in his boat for rides.
The fishes of course were very pleased about this.

So now in summer Fabian helps his father in the vineyards.
He takes the little boys from the village to the beach
and teaches them how to swim.
He is happy if, between two waves, he catches a glimpse
of one of his friends passing by, peacefully and without haste,
because they are not afraid anymore.
But sometimes he thinks back with longing to the time
when he still was a real fish-boy —
especially in the evenings, when he has to leave the water to
run,
    sit,
        blow his nose,
            scratch behind the ear,
                eat from a plate,
                    sleep in a bed,
                        go to school,
and — to pull the cat's tail.